THIS BOOK
BELONGS TO

_____

KARA'S CHRISTMAS SMILE

A. M. Marcus

Kara woke on the morning of Christmas Eve. She had been hoping for a cat for Christmas but there were no more in the pet shop.

Kara's mom said she could have a toy cat instead, so off they went to buy some Christmas gifts and the new toy.

5

In the store, people were complaining about the long queues, but Kara was just excited to be shopping with her mom.

Kara loved looking at all the toys and then finally she saw the perfect toy kitten. It was the very last one.

When she turned to ask her mom to buy it for her, she noticed a young boy staring at the kitten in her arms.

He was sad because he wanted the kitten too.

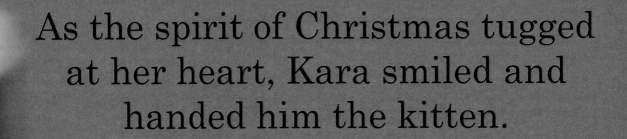

As the spirit of Christmas tugged at her heart, Kara smiled and handed him the kitten.

The boy's eyes lit up, and he grinned. "Thank you!" he cried and ran off to tell his mom.

As he was leaving the store, he noticed a lady had dropped her purse and her money was scattered all over the floor.

The boy was excited about going home to play with his new toy, but as he looked at the toy in his arms he thought about the kindness of the girl. He smiled as he bent down to help the lady. She couldn't help but smile back.

As the woman was waiting
to pay for her presents,
a man and his son were
behind her in the queue.

The little boy was crying,
and his dad was trying to
calm him down.

The woman was still smiling as she thought about how the little boy had helped her.

She turned to the father and son and asked if they would like to go ahead of her in the queue. The father smiled back in relief "Thank you" he said.

As the father and his son left the store, they saw an elderly woman slip on the ice and fall.

Seeing that she needed help, they stopped and offered to take her to a nearby medical clinic. The eledery woman was very grateful for the ride.

Inside the clinic, the nurse was feeling sad that she had to work on Christmas Eve and couldn't be home with her family.

Feeling grateful, the elderly woman saw the nurse's sad eyes and wanted to cheer her up.

She smiled at the nurse and
handed her some candy.

When her last patient left, the nurse walked out into the cold to head home. As she wrapped her coat tightly around herself, she noticed a girl shivering.

24

As the nurse remembered the kindness of the eledery woman, she took off her coat and placed it over the girl's shoulders with a smile.

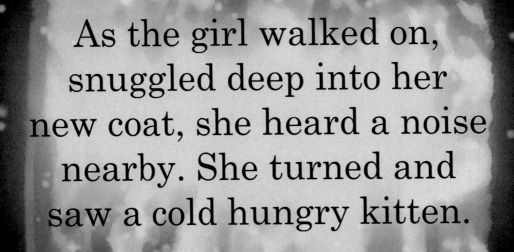

As the girl walked on, snuggled deep into her new coat, she heard a noise nearby. She turned and saw a cold hungry kitten.

Feeling thankful for her warm coat, the girl decided to feed the cold hungry kitten. She smiled as she fed it some tuna from her sandwich.

The kitten purred happily and
headed down the sidewalk
looking for a shelter for the night.

As the kitten walked,
it bumped straight into
Kara, who was just
finishing the last of her
Christmas shopping.
Kara turned just in time
to see the kitten sitting
next to her.

"Look, Mommy!" Kara cried, scooping up the tiny kitten. "It has no collar and it's out all alone in the cold. Can we take it home?"

"I think that's a great idea!" said Kara's mom. Kara cuddled her new pet and smiled.

Mark's Mystery Message

☐   Did you ever do a kind thing for someone else?

☐   Can you remember a time when someone did something kind for you? What did they do?

☐   If you do a kind thing for someone, how do you think they will feel?

☐   What kind of things do you think they might do if they feel this way?

☐   What can you do today to start a chain of kindness?

 **What Do You Think The Message Is?**

The Message

Free

ACTiVitY
PACK 3

The Self-Esteem Series

My Favorite...

FRUIT: Strawberry

SCHOOL SUBJECT: Math

HOBBY: Dancing

COLOR: Green

ANIMAL: Tiger

SPORT: Soccer

PET: Dog

What's Your Favorite?

"Too often we underestimate the power of a touch, a smile, a kind word, a listening ear, an honest compliment, or the smallest act of caring, all of which have the potential to turn a life around."

– Leo Buscaglia

By A. M. Marcus

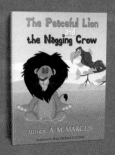

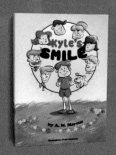

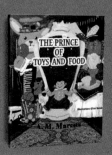

www.ammarcus.com

For The Grown Ups...

Thank you for sharing this story with your children, I hope you find it useful!

The questions that appear at the end of the story were engineered to be used chronologically to lead young people step by step to take ownership of the message in the quote by Leo Buscaglia.

As a parent, raising a smiling, caring, and kind child who truly cares for others is both a privilege and a challenge. I hope you found this story to be a fun, light-hearted way to show children the power of kindness, and how a simple smile can have a ripple effect, bringing happiness to a whole community. I often like to remind myself how powerful a smile can be.

If you also enjoyed the message of this story, please consider sharing it with a friend or on social media. Your help in spreading the word is greatly appreciated. Together we can make a huge difference in helping new readers find children's books with powerful messages similar to the one in this story.

If you would like to learn more about me or you have any questions, I would love to hear from you.
You can contact me via my website at <u>ammarcus.com/contact</u> or simply send me an email to <u>assaf@ammarcus.com</u>

My message to the world can be summarised in TWO WORDS.

Visit my website to see what they are 😉

Scan For Your Free Gift

Use the code
09189

ammarcus/free-gift

Made in the USA
Middletown, DE
09 December 2019